# Calinours

*fait la fête*

Dans la clairière,
près du grand buisson,
qui pousse une brouette
en revenant vers sa maison ?

ISBN 978-2-211-20547-4
Première édition dans la collection *lutin poche* : mai 2011
© 2009, l'école des loisirs, Paris
Loi numéro 49 956 du 16 juillet 1949 sur les publications
destinées à la jeunesse : mars 2009
Dépôt légal : mai 2011
Imprimé en France par Mame à Tours

Alain Broutin

# Calinours

## *fait la fête*

illustré par Frédéric Stehr

lutin poche de l'école des loisirs

11, rue de Sèvres, Paris 6ᵉ

« Coucou ! C'est moi, Calinours !
Je suis avec mes amis, monsieur Rossignol,
papy Papillon, mademoiselle l'Abeille, et ils me parlent à l'oreille.
Ma brouette est vide mais dedans, il y avait… »
« Chut ! » dit monsieur Rossignol, « c'est encore un grand secret. »

« Monsieur Rossignol,
maintenant, ouvre tes ailes,
et vole à travers la forêt
pour annoncer la nouvelle. »

Monsieur Rossignol s'envole. Il chante à tue-tête :
« Ohé ! Ohé ! Calinours veut faire la fête !
Tout le monde se déguise,
rendez-vous dans la clairière, il y aura des surprises ! »

C'est l'heure de la fête.
Les invités qui arrivent s'amusent à se reconnaître.
Celui-là, qui peut-il être ?
Un grand chapeau, un long manteau, une baguette…
Les amis rigolent : « Hi ! Hi ! Hi ! Le grand magicien,
on t'a reconnu, petit coquin. »

« Oui, c'est moi », dit Calinours.
« Je vous reconnais aussi.
Hi ! Hi ! Hi ! La grande sauterelle,
madame Grenouille, je t'ai reconnue.
Ha ! Ha ! Ha ! La grosse coccinelle,
reconnue, madame Tortue.

Hi! Hi! Hi! Le canard poilu,
monsieur Renard, je t'ai reconnu.
Ha! Ha! Ha! La souris qui vole,
reconnu, monsieur Rossignol.»

Soudain, tous les bruits s'arrêtent.
Le grand magicien vient de lever sa baguette.
En soulevant son grand chapeau, Calinours s'écrie :

« Abracadabra ! Que les petites abeilles bourdonnent ! »
« Quelle merveille ! » disent les amis.
« Les petites abeilles bourdonnent,
et ça fait un soleil qui tourbillonne. »

En ouvrant son long manteau, Calinours s'écrie :
« Abracadabra ! Que les papillons papillonnent ! »
« Quelle merveille ! » disent les amis.

« Les papillons
papillonnent,
maintenant,
le soleil rayonne. »

17

Calinours dit : « Dansons autour du soleil.
Un pas en avant, on se tient par les papattes.
Deux pas en arrière…

On tombe tous sur le derrière. »
« Oh ! » s'écrie madame Tortue,
« quand on est par terre, le soleil éclate. »
« Oui », dit Calinours. « Pour qu'il brille encore,
il faut se lever et crier très fort : Soleil, où es-tu ? »

Assis, debout, on rit, on danse,
et on crie : « Soleil, où es-tu ? »
Debout, assis, on recommence...

Tout à coup, Calinours gonfle ses joues.
Il souffle sur le soleil : Fwou ! Fwou !
Le soleil s'enfuit.
Calinours court après lui.

Monsieur Castor dit :
« Ils sont près du grand buisson, allons-y !
Je sens quelque chose d'étrange. »
« Et moi », dit madame Souris,
« je suis sûre que ça se mange. »

« Regardez ! » crie monsieur Castor.
« Derrière le buisson,
il y a un trésor,
plein de tartelettes.
Mais qui les a faites ? »

« C'est moi », dit Calinours en riant,
« et je les ai même transportées dans ma brouette. »

À chacun sa part.
Une tartelette aux poires
pour monsieur Renard
et une aux poireaux
pour monsieur Blaireau.
Une à la citrouille
pour madame Grenouille
et une à l'andouille
pour monsieur Crapaud.
Et la tarte au miel…
c'est pour le Soleil.

Mais tout à coup…
Biz biz biz ! Les petites abeilles bourdonnent.
Zou zou zou ! Les papillons papillonnent.
« Quelle merveille ! » dit Calinours.
« Biz biz biz et zou zou zou,
ça me fait tout plein de petits bisous. »

« Calinours, merci ! merci ! »
s'écrient les amis.
« La fête est très réussie !
Petit soleil, bravo ! Bravo !
Il n'a jamais fait aussi beau ! »

# Forces

Harcourt

SCHOOL PUBLISHERS

Orlando   Austin   New York   San Diego   Toronto   London

Visit *The Learning Site!*
**www.harcourtschool.com**

# What Forces Affect Objects on Earth Every Day?

**VOCABULARY**

force
friction
gravity
gravitational force
magnetism
magnetic force

A **force** is a push or pull that causes motion. The boy in the picture applied a force to the dominoes. The force knocked them over.

**Friction** is a force that can make things slow down, stop, or not move at all. Friction between the ice and skate helps the skater stop.

2

**Gravity** is the force of attraction between two objects. The picture shows that gravity attracts the feather and the apple.

Earth has a large **gravitational force** because it has a lot of mass.

**Magnetic force** is the force produced by a magnet. Earth is like a big magnet. In the picture, you can see the magnetic field around Earth.

**READING FOCUS SKILL**
**CAUSE AND EFFECT**

A **cause** makes something happen. An **effect** is what happens.

Look for the **cause** of changes in objects. Also look for the **effects** of the changes.

# Forces

A **force** is a push or pull that causes motion. Many different forces push and pull you all the time. One force pulls you down to Earth when you jump up. Another force makes two magnets stick together.

A force can speed things up, slow them down, or make them change direction.

In the picture, the dominoes stand still until the boy pushes them over. His push is the force that starts the first domino in motion.

 **Tell what will happen to the other dominoes after the boy pushes over the first domino.**

# Friction

When skates dig into the ice, the skater slows down. When a soccer ball rolls across the grass, it slows down.

The force that makes things slow down is called **friction**. Friction can even stop something or keep it from moving at all. Friction opposes motion. You have friction any time two surfaces touch.

Friction can also make heat. Rub your hands together. The heat you feel is caused by friction.

Friction is greater between rough surfaces than between smooth surfaces. Have you ever "sock skated"? You can glide across a smooth, waxed surface in your socks. This is because there is not much friction. Take your socks off, or try an unwaxed wood floor. You won't go very far. Friction is greater.

 **Tell why a soccer ball slows down as it rolls.**

# Gravity

The force of attraction between two objects is called **gravity**. All objects have some gravity. But larger objects, like a planet, have more gravity. When you fall out of your chair, Earth's gravity is what pulls you to the ground. Earth's gravity makes something fall to the floor if you drop it.

Gravity also causes falling objects to speed up. Look at the picture below. The photographs were taken split seconds apart. At first, the apple and feather each fell a short distance. Later, they fell a longer distance. This shows that they fell faster at the bottom of the picture. They sped up. Gravity caused the objects to speed up as they fell.

All objects in the universe, large and small, pull at one another. This pulling is called **gravitational force**. The strength of this force depends on two things. One is the distance between the objects. The force is stronger when objects are near each other. The other thing is the objects' mass, or amount of matter. The force is stronger when objects have more mass.

Earth has more mass than the moon. So the Earth pulls on objects with more gravitational force.

A person will weigh more on Earth than on the moon. The person's mass remains the same. But the weight changes. This is because weight is a measure of the amount of gravitational force pulling on an object.

 **Tell why a person weighs more on Earth than on the moon.**

The moon has less mass than Earth, so it has less gravitational force. On the moon, objects weigh about one-sixth of what they weigh on Earth. ▶

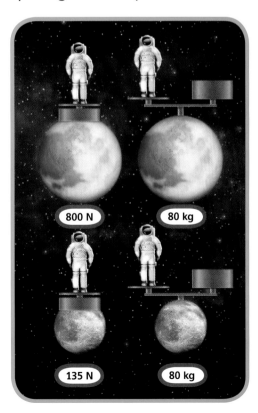

800 N   80 kg

135 N   80 kg

# Magnetism

Have you ever picked up paper clips with a magnet? The force produced by a magnet is called **magnetic force**. A magnet is surrounded by a magnetic field. This is what attracts objects.

A magnet has two ends, called poles. The magnetic field is strongest at these poles.

Earth is like a big magnet. Its poles are called the North Pole and the South Pole.

**A magnetic field fills the space around Earth.** ▼

An ordinary magnet has a north-seeking pole and a south-seeking pole. This means that the north-seeking pole will point north. The south-seeking pole will point south.

A compass needle is a magnet. Its north-seeking pole always points toward Earth's North Pole. A compass can help people know which direction they are going.

You hold one magnet's north-seeking pole to another magnet's north-seeking pole. They push away from each other. But a magnet's north-seeking pole will attract another magnet's south-seeking pole.

 **Why does a compass help you find direction?**

**Fill in these cause and effect statements.**

1. A _____ is a push or pull that causes motion.

2. _____ is the force that causes things to fall toward Earth.

3. Friction makes a soccer ball _____ _____ as it rolls across the grass.

4. Magnetism causes a compass needle to point toward the _____ Pole.

5. A person will weigh _____ on the moon than on Earth because the moon has less mass.

9

# What Are Balanced and Unbalanced Forces?

**VOCABULARY**

balanced forces
unbalanced
    forces
net force
buoyant force

When two forces act equally on an object but in opposite directions, the object does not move. The forces are **balanced forces**. In the picture, the rope is not moving. This is because the teams are pulling equally in opposite directions. If one team pulls harder than the other, the forces will be **unbalanced forces**. The rope will move in the direction of the team that pulls harder.

When you add all the forces acting on an object, you get the **net force**. In the picture, all the forces are acting in the same direction.

The force of water pushing up on an object is called the **buoyant force**.

When you compare and contrast, you find what is alike and different between two things.

Find what is alike and different about balanced and unbalanced forces.

# Balanced and Unbalanced Forces

Usually more than one force is acting on an object. When you go down a slide, gravity is acting on you to make you move. Friction is acting on you to slow you down. When the force of gravity is equal to the force of friction, you stop. The two forces are balanced. The forces cancel each other. When the forces acting on an object cancel each other, they are called **balanced forces**.

The forces are balanced, so the dresser does not move. ▼

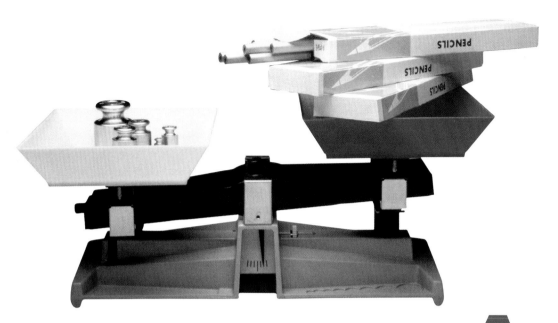

If you give yourself a push going down a slide, you start moving again. The forces become **unbalanced forces**. In the picture above, the weights on one side of the balance are heavier. They go down. You can see that the forces are unbalanced.

The two pictures below show balanced forces. What could happen to make these forces become unbalanced?

 **Tell how balanced forces are different from unbalanced forces.**

# Net Force

Remember that many forces are acting on an object all the time. All these forces together are called the **net force**.

Net force affects how an object moves. If you know the net force, you know how the object moves. You don't have to know the details of all the forces acting on an object.

When forces are balanced, the net force is zero. Look at the deer in the picture below. Each deer is pushing with equal force. One deer is pushing to the left. One deer is pushing to the right. The forces are balanced. The deer are not moving. The net force is zero.

**A net force of zero means the forces are balanced.** ▼

When the forces acting on an object are unbalanced, the net force is not zero. When forces are unbalanced, motion results. Look at the picture of the wrestlers. The one on the right is pushing with more force. He is pushing the other wrestler to the left. Since the forces are unbalanced, the wrestlers will move to the left.

When all the forces acting on an object are acting in the same direction, you find the net force by adding all the forces together.

 **Tell how balanced and unbalanced forces affect net force.**

The net force is the sum of all the forces. When forces act in the same direction, find the net force by adding the individual forces. ▶

# Buoyant Force

When you are in the water, you seem to weigh less. This is because a force acts on your body. The force pushes you up. This force is called a **buoyant force**. A buoyant force acts in the opposite direction from weight. Weight is the measure of gravity pulling down on you. A buoyant force pushes you up, so you seem to weigh less.

A buoyant force helps you float. When you get into the water, your body pushes the water aside. If the buoyant force is equal to or greater than the weight of the water you push aside, you will float. If the buoyant force is less than the weight of the water you push aside, you will sink.

**A buoyant force pushes up on the duck. Since the force is equal to or greater than the weight of the water the duck displaces, the duck floats. ▼**

buoyant force

weight

In the picture below, the ball of clay sinks. But the clay boat floats. The same amount of clay is used for each object.

The ball of clay is heavier than the water it pushes aside. So it sinks. But the boy reshaped the other piece of clay. The clay now pushes aside enough water to equal its weight. So the clay boat floats.

 **Tell how two objects with the same mass can be affected differently by the buoyant force.**

The clay boat floats, but the clay ball sinks. ▶

## Review

**Complete these compare and contrast statements.**

1. When forces are balanced, an object does not _____.

2. When forces are balanced, the net force is _____.

3. When forces are unbalanced, an object will _____.

4. When all the forces acting on an object are acting in the same direction, you find the net force by _____ the forces together.

# What Is Work, and How Is It Measured?

**VOCABULARY**

work
simple machine
lever
fulcrum
inclined plane
pulley
wheel-and-axle
compound
  machine

In science, **work** means using a force to move an object. Lifting a bucket of water is an example of work.

Sometimes people use a **simple machine** to make work easier. One type of simple machine is an **inclined plane**. A ramp is an inclined plane.

18

A **wheel-and-axle** is a simple machine. It is made of a wheel with a rod through the center. The rod is called an axle.

A **pulley** is a wheel with a groove for a rope. A dumb-waiter uses a pulley to lift a heavy load.

A **lever** is a bar that makes moving things easier. The bar has a **fulcrum**, or balance point.

**READING FOCUS SKILL**
**MAIN IDEA AND DETAILS**

The **main idea** is what the text is mostly about. **Details** are pieces of information about the **main idea**.

Look for what work is and **details** about how people make work easier.

## Work

In science, work has a special meaning. To do **work**, you must use a force to move an object. Pushing a box across a floor is work. Reading a book is not. Lifting a bucket is work. Doing a math problem in your head is not. The boy in the picture applies force to the bowling ball to move it. He is doing work.

 **What is work?**

▼ To do work, you must move an object.

# Machines and Work

A machine is something that makes work easier. This means you can do more work with less force. A **simple machine** can change the size or direction of the force. Or it can change the distance the object travels.

A **lever** is a simple machine. It is a bar that makes moving things easier. A lever has two parts. The lever arm is the bar. This is the part you hold. The **fulcrum** is the balance point that supports the bar.

An **inclined plane** is also a simple machine. It is a sloping surface, like a ramp. You use less force, but you go a longer distance.

**A ramp is an inclined plane. A wedge is an inclined plane that you can move. A chisel is a wedge.** ▼

Chisel

Lever

21

Another kind of simple machine is a pulley. A **pulley** is a wheel with a groove for a rope. A pulley can help you lift a heavy object. It lets you pull on the rope instead of pushing up on the object.

A **wheel-and-axle** is a simple machine made of a wheel and a rod. The rod, or axle, goes through the center of the wheel. A doorknob is a wheel-and-axle. A potter's wheel is also a wheel-and-axle.

 **Tell how you use simple machines.**

A potter uses a wheel-and-axle. ▶

# Compound Machines

A **compound machine** is made up of two or more simple machines. It also makes work easier. Usually, it makes work easier by letting you use less force over a greater distance.

One type of compound machine is a can opener. It has a wedge that cuts into the can. It has a wheel-and-axle that you turn.

 **Tell how people use compound machines to make work easier.**

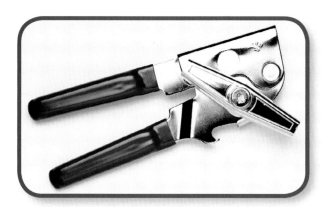

◄ A can opener is a compound machine.

 **Review**

**Complete this main idea statement.**

1. People use _____ _____ to make work easier.

**Complete these detail statements.**

2. A _____ is made of a bar and a fulcrum.

3. A _____ _____ is made of two or more simple machines.

4. A doorknob is an example of a _____.

# GLOSSARY

**balanced forces** (BAL•uhnst FAWRS•iz) forces that act on an object but cancel each other out.

**buoyant force** (BOY•uhnt FAWRS) the upward force exerted on an object by water.

**force** (FAWRS) a push or pull that causes an object to move, stop, or change direction.

**friction** (FRIK•shuhn) a force that opposes motion.

**fulcrum** (FUHL•kruhm) the balance point on a lever that supports the arm but does not move.

**gravitational force** (grav•ih•TAY•shuhn•uhl FAWRS) the pull of all objects in the universe on one another.

**gravity** (GRAV•ih•tee) the force of attraction between objects.

**inclined plane** (in•KLYND PLAYN) a ramp or another sloping surface.

**lever** (LEV•er) a bar that makes it easier to move things.

**magnetic force** (mag•NE•tik FAWRS) the force produced by a magnet.

**net force** (NET FAWRS) the combination of all the forces acting on an object.

**pulley** (PUHL•ee) a wheel with a rope that lets you change the direction in which you apply force.

**simple machine** (SIM•puhl muh•SHEEN) a device that makes a task easier by changing the size or direction of a force or the distance over which the force acts.

**unbalanced forces** (uhn•BAL•uhnst FAWRS•iz) forces that act on an object and don't cancel each other out; unbalanced forces cause a change in motion.

**wheel-and-axle** (weel•and•AK•suhl) a wheel with a rod, or axle, in the center.

**work** (WERK) the use of a force to move an object through a distance.